Conten

Age-Appropriate Skills

Language

- following directions
- story comprehension
- descriptive and comparative language
- rhyming
- categorization
- letter recognition and phonemic awareness
- statements and questions
- auditory and visual discrimination
- left-to-right tracking
- oral language
- vocabulary and concept development
- sequencing
- color words

Math

- counting to 20
- patterning
- numeral recognition
- geometric shapes
- beginning computation
- one-to-one matching
- graphing
- measurement

Dear Parent,

The stories in this book have themes related to your child's body, how your child grows and changes, and how to be healthy and strong. Use the stories to introduce vocabulary and concepts related to your child's body.

Reading stories aloud will help your child develop a love of reading, and it has proven to enhance a variety of early language skills, including:

- letter recognition and phonemic awareness,
- auditory and visual discrimination,
- left-to-right tracking, and
- vocabulary and concept development.

As you read to your child, remember to:

- speak clearly and with interest.
- track words by moving your finger under each word as you read it.
- ask your child to identify objects in the pictures. Talk about these objects together.
- allow your child to express his or her own thoughts and ideas and to ask you questions.

Support and guide your child as he or she completes the activities. Recognize the efforts your child has made and encourage your child as he or she learns to master basic skills.

We hope your child enjoys these stories and activities.

Sincerely,
Evan-Moor Educational Publishers

My Body

Look at me.
What do you see?

Early Bird: Body • EMC 7054 •

1 head,

1 chest,

1 tummy,

and 1 seat,

2

2 arms,

2 hands,

2 legs,

and 2 feet,

3

Early Bird: Body • EMC 7054 • © Evan-Moor Corp.

all covered by my skin.

4

Look inside me.
What do you see?

Early Bird: Body • EMC 7054 • © Evan-Moor Corp.

1 brain and 1 heart,

6

2 lungs and 1 stomach,

Early Bird: Body • EMC 7054 • © Evan-Moor Corp.

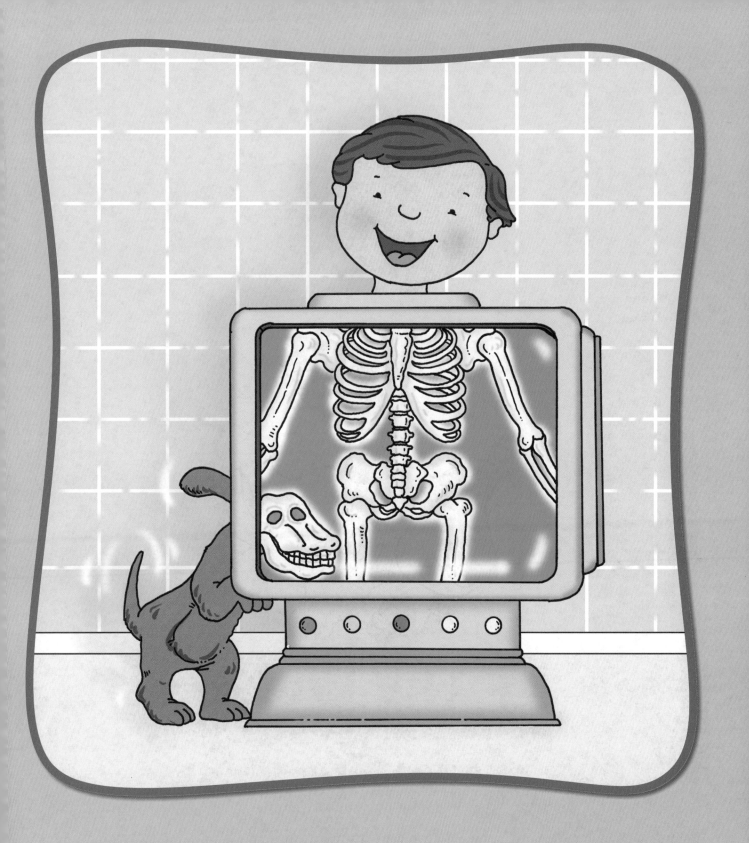

and a skeleton to hold them all in.

8

The End

Early Bird: Body • EMC 7054 • © Evan-Moor Corp.

Note: Review "My Body" circle-time story. Children color the parts of the human body and cross out the parts of an animal body.

Story Comprehension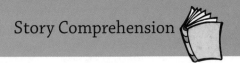

My Body

Color the boy's body parts.

Draw an **X** on any dog body parts.

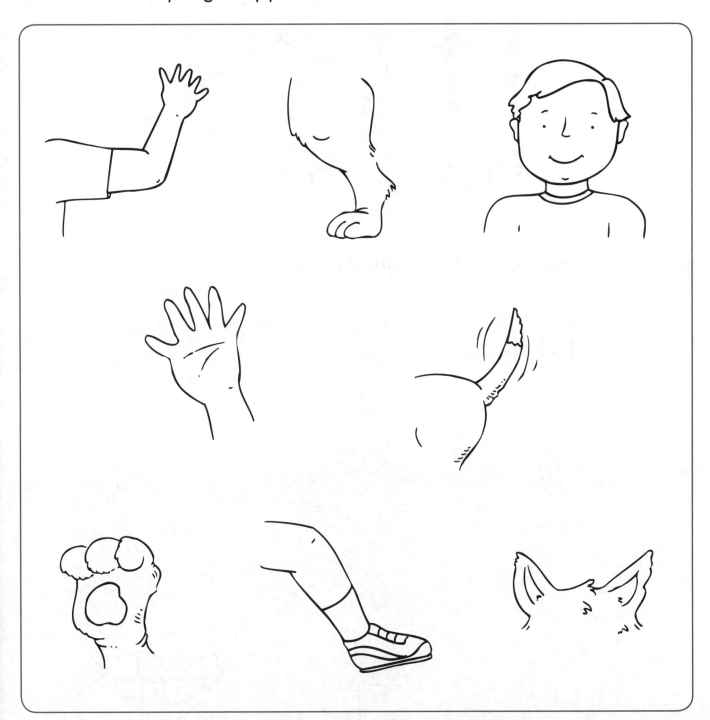

Note: Children think of things in the classroom that begin with the same sound as *face*. Then they color the pictures that begin with that same sound.

It Starts Like Face

Color the face.

Color the pictures that begin the same as **face**.

Early Bird: Body • EMC 7054 • © Evan-Moor Corp.

Note: After reviewing rhyming words, children circle the pictures that rhyme with *toes*.

Language—Rhyming Words

It Rhymes with Toes

Circle the pictures that rhyme with **toes**.

  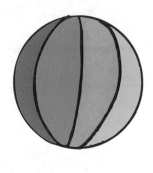

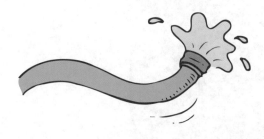  

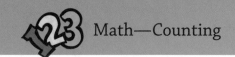

Note: Children write the numbers 1 through 10 on the fingers and toes.

Fingers and Toes

Write the numbers 1–10 on the fingers and toes.

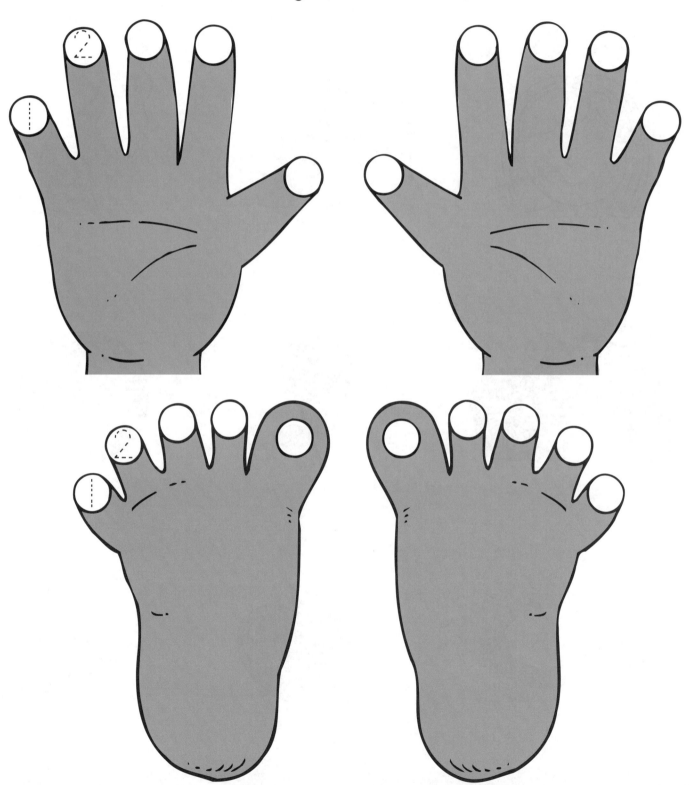

I Grow and Change

Bringing home baby!

Bath time

Christmas

This is my handprint
when I was a baby.

This is my handprint now.
My body grows and changes.

2

These were my shoes
when I was a baby.

These are my shoes now.
My body grows and changes.

This was my shirt
when I was a baby.

This is my shirt now.
My body grows and changes.

This is me when I was a baby.

And this is me now.
My body grows and changes.

8

The End

Note: Children cut out the pictures, color them, and glue them in the correct column.

Story Comprehension

Is It Mine?

Color.  Cut. Glue.

glue	glue
glue	glue
glue	glue

Note: Read the directions to the children. Children color the boxes that contain the word *grow*.

Language—Word Recognition

Growing Up

Help the baby grow into a big boy.
Color the boxes that have the word **grow**.

grow	big	big	baby	small
grow	big	small	hop	big
grow	grow	small	baby	hop
chick	grow	grow	grow	big
small	big	baby	grow	barn
hop	big	small	grow	grow

Note: Children count the number of items that do not have an **X** and write the correct number in the box.

How Many Are Left?

Count. Write.

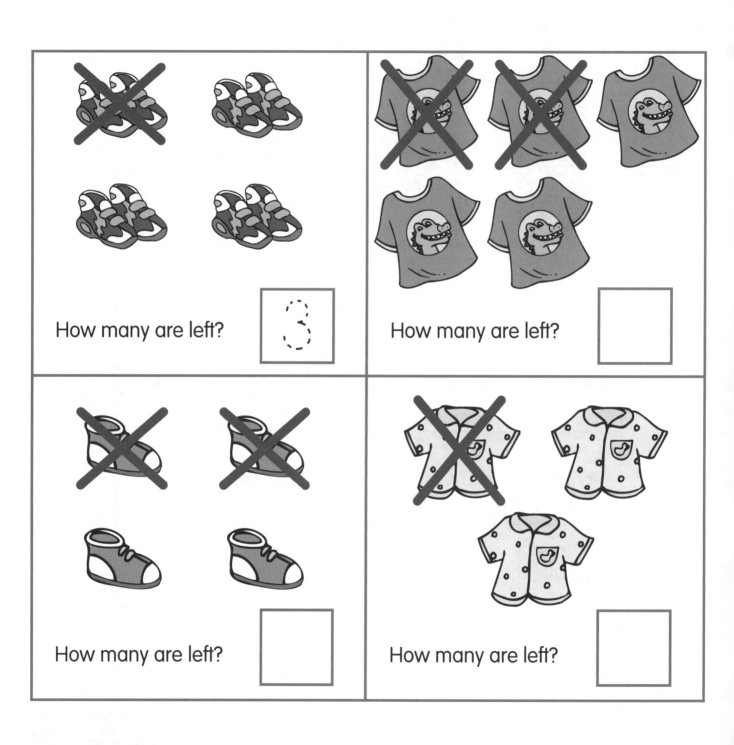

How many are left?   3

How many are left?

How many are left?

How many are left?

Early Bird: Body • EMC 7054 • © Evan-Moor Corp.

Note: Review the name of each item with children. Children cut out the pictures, color them, and glue them in the correct column.

Language—Categorization

What Do I Use?

Color. Cut. Glue.

glue	glue	glue	glue
glue	glue	glue	glue

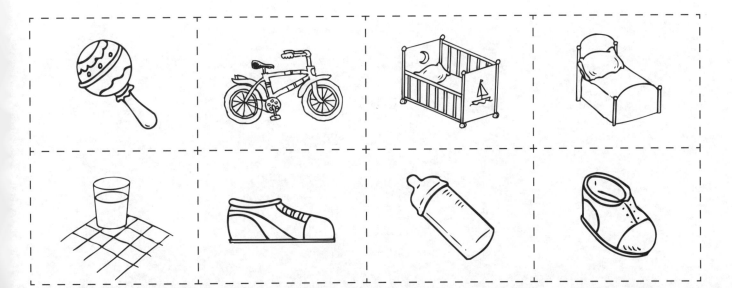

Healthy and Strong

Sally eats a good breakfast.
She eats healthy snacks, too.
She knows that eating right
is the thing to do.

It keeps her body healthy and strong.

1

Sally washes her hands.
She takes a bath, too.
She knows that keeping clean
is the thing to do.

It keeps her body healthy and strong.

2

Sally plays with her friends.
She plays with her family, too.
She knows that getting exercise
is the thing to do.

It keeps her body healthy and strong.

3

Sally rests when she's tired.
She sleeps all night, too.
She knows that getting rest
is the thing to do.

It keeps her body healthy and strong.

4

Sally brushes her teeth.
She flosses them, too.
She knows that cleaning her teeth
is the thing to do.

It keeps her body healthy and strong.

5

Early Bird: Body • EMC 7054 • © Evan-Moor Corp.

Sally goes to the dentist.

6

She goes to the doctor, too.
She knows that getting checkups
is the thing to do.

It keeps her body healthy and strong.

7

Can you keep your body
healthy and strong, too?
What should you do?

8

The End

Note: Children figure out what each child needs and then trace the path from the child to the correct spot.

Language—Tracking

What Do I Need?

Trace each line.

It Starts Like Wash

Color the pictures that begin the same as **wash**.

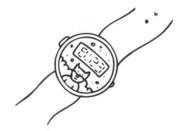

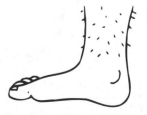

Note: Children cut out and glue the correct pictures to complete each pattern.

Finish the Patterns

Cut.

Glue.

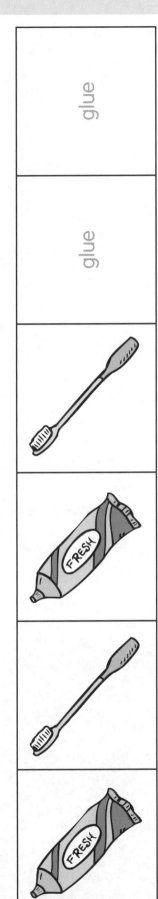

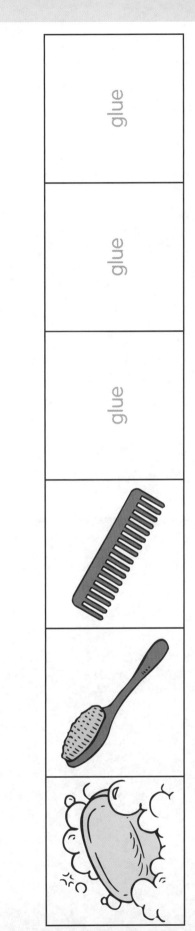

Note: Review the names of the shapes below. Children use the color key to correctly color the picture below.

Color the Shapes

Color.

brown   blue   red

Alphabet Cards

Use these colorful alphabet cards in a variety of ways. Simply laminate and cut apart the cards and store them in a sturdy envelope or box.

Alphabet cards can be used to practice skills such as:

- letter recognition
- letter-sound association
- visual perception

Alphabet Card Games ······································

What's My Name?	Use the alphabet cards to introduce the names of the letters, both uppercase and lowercase.
Make a Match	Children match a lowercase and uppercase letter. They then turn the cards over to self-check. If a correct match has been made, the child will see a picture of the same object, whose name begins with the letter being matched.
First-Sound Game	Use the alphabet cards as phonics flashcards and ask children to identify the sound of each letter.
ABC Order	Children take all of the uppercase or lowercase cards and place them in alphabetical order.

A a

B b

C c

D d

apple

Apple

bath

Bath

carrot

Carrot

dog

Dog

E

e

F

f

G

g

H

h

egg

Egg

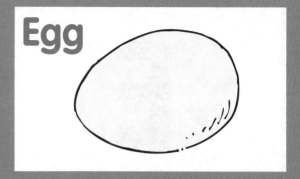

foot

Foot

girl

Girl

helmet

Helmet

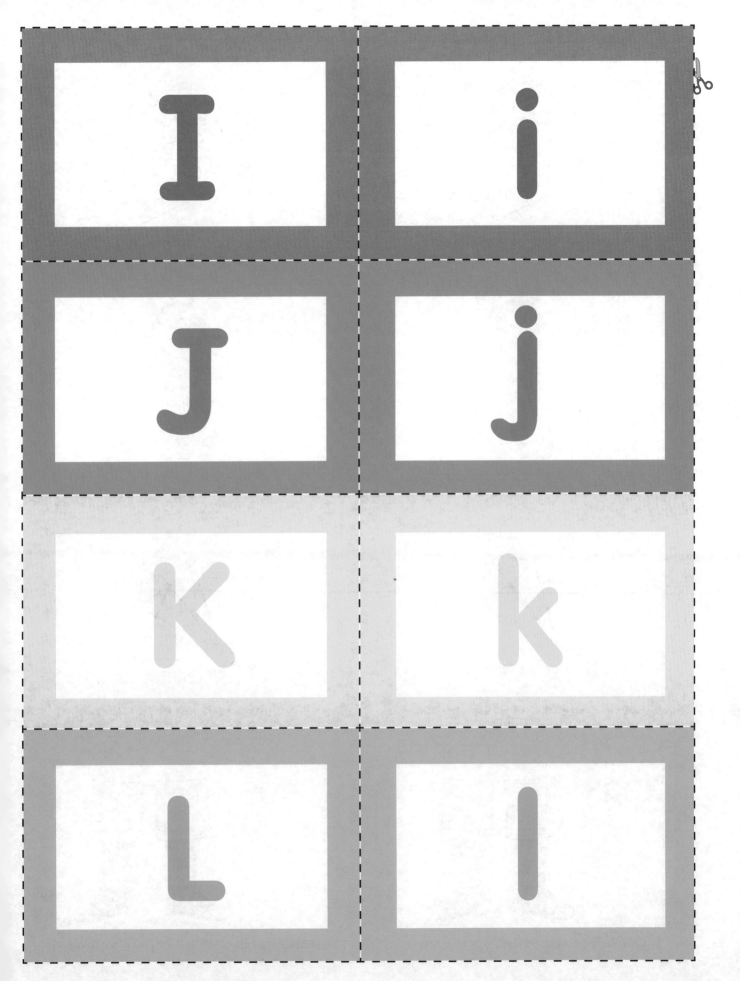

I   i

J   j

K   k

L   l

in

Early Bird: Body • EMC 7054 • © Evan-Moor Corp.

In

Early Bird: Body • EMC 7054 • © Evan-Moor Corp.

jump

Early Bird: Body • EMC 7054 • © Evan-Moor Corp.

Jump

Early Bird: Body • EMC 7054 • © Evan-Moor Corp.

kite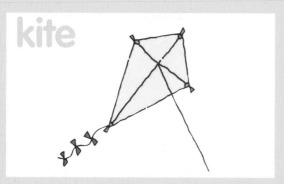

Early Bird: Body • EMC 7054 • © Evan-Moor Corp.

Kite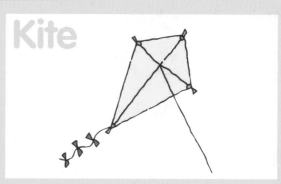

Early Bird: Body • EMC 7054 • © Evan-Moor Corp.

legs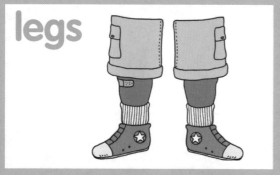

Early Bird: Body • EMC 7054 • © Evan-Moor Corp.

Legs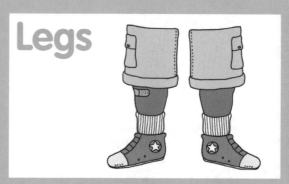

Early Bird: Body • EMC 7054 • © Evan-Moor Corp.

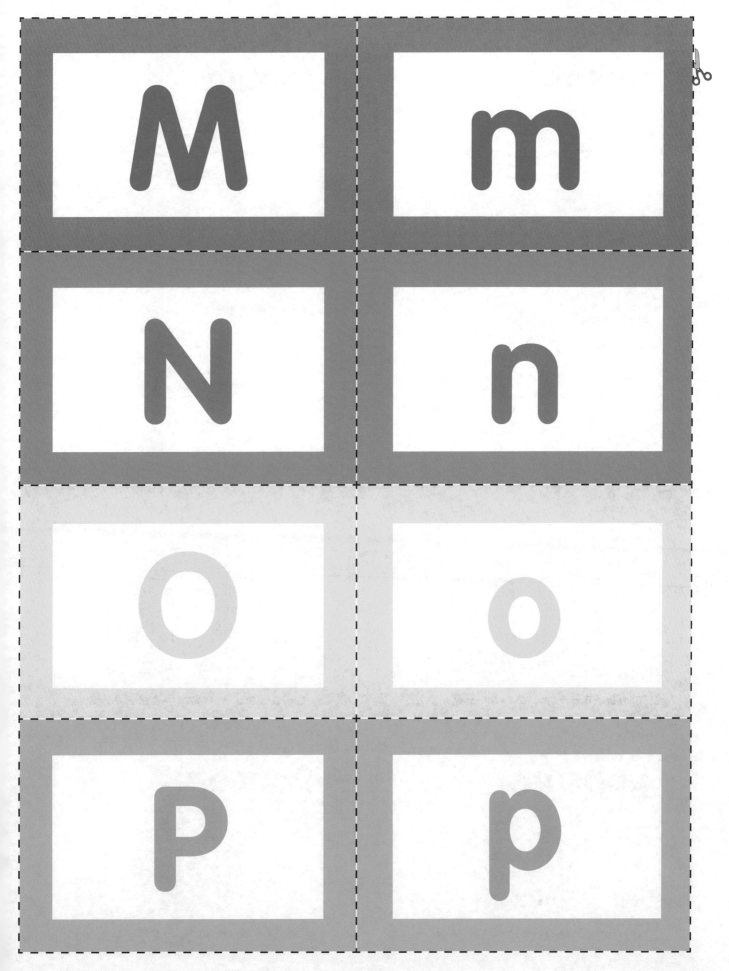

mouth

Early Bird: Body • EMC 7054 • © Evan-Moor Corp.

Mouth

Early Bird: Body • EMC 7054 • © Evan-Moor Corp.

nose

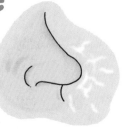

Early Bird: Body • EMC 7054 • © Evan-Moor Corp.

Nose

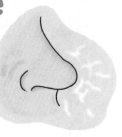

Early Bird: Body • EMC 7054 • © Evan-Moor Corp.

on/off

Early Bird: Body • EMC 7054 • © Evan-Moor Corp.

On/Off

Early Bird: Body • EMC 7054 • © Evan-Moor Corp.

popcorn

Early Bird: Body • EMC 7054 • © Evan-Moor Corp.

Popcorn

Early Bird: Body • EMC 7054 • © Evan-Moor Corp.

Q   q

R   r

S   s

T   t

quiet shh...

Early Bird: Body • EMC 7054 • © Evan-Moor Corp.

Quiet shh...

Early Bird: Body • EMC 7054 • © Evan-Moor Corp.

ride

Early Bird: Body • EMC 7054 • © Evan-Moor Corp.

Ride

Early Bird: Body • EMC 7054 • © Evan-Moor Corp.

sun

Early Bird: Body • EMC 7054 • © Evan-Moor Corp.

Sun

Early Bird: Body • EMC 7054 • © Evan-Moor Corp.

teeth

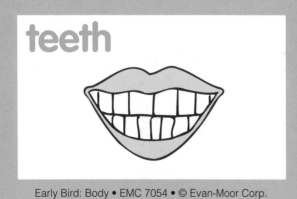

Early Bird: Body • EMC 7054 • © Evan-Moor Corp.

Teeth

Early Bird: Body • EMC 7054 • © Evan-Moor Corp.

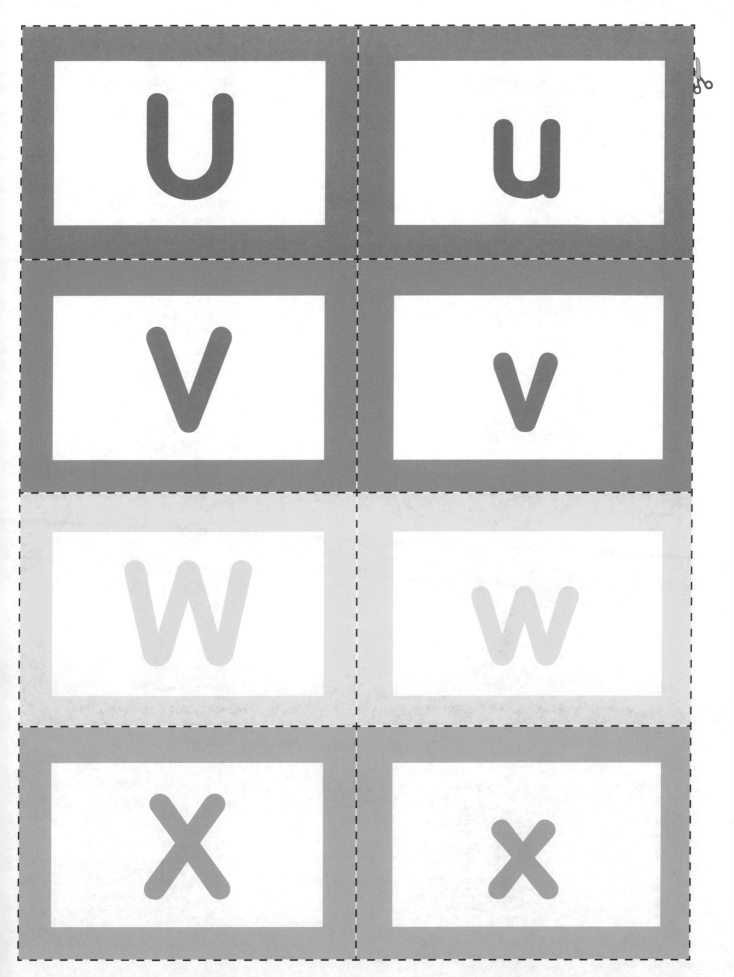

U u

V v

W w

X x

us

Early Bird: Body • EMC 7054 • © Evan-Moor Corp.

Us

Early Bird: Body • EMC 7054 • © Evan-Moor Corp.

vegetables

Early Bird: Body • EMC 7054 • © Evan-Moor Corp.

Vegetables

Early Bird: Body • EMC 7054 • © Evan-Moor Corp.

walk

Early Bird: Body • EMC 7054 • © Evan-Moor Corp.

Walk

Early Bird: Body • EMC 7054 • © Evan-Moor Corp.

x-ray

Early Bird: Body • EMC 7054 • © Evan-Moor Corp.

X-ray

Early Bird: Body • EMC 7054 • © Evan-Moor Corp.

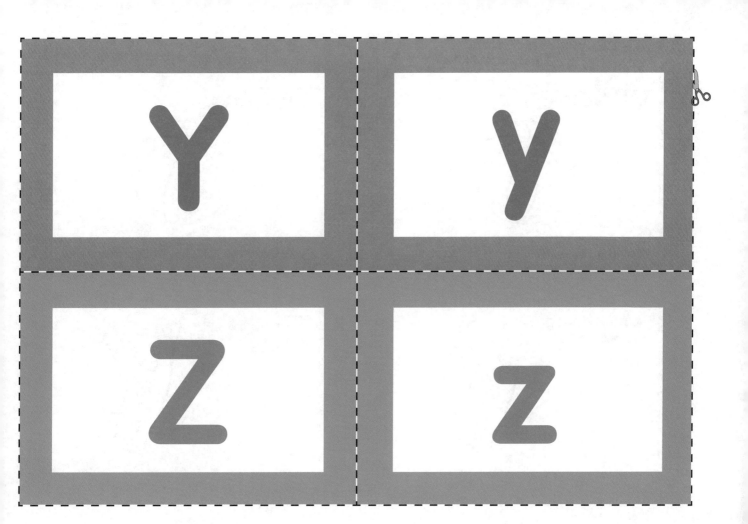

yellow

Yellow

zipper

Zipper

Answer Key

Page 13

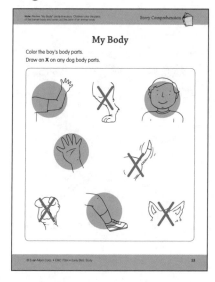

Page 14

Page 15

Page 16

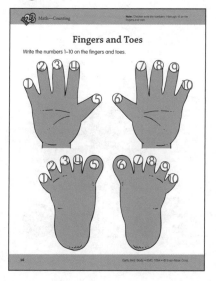

Page 27

Page 29

Page 30

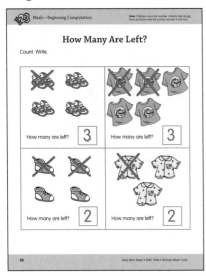

Page 31

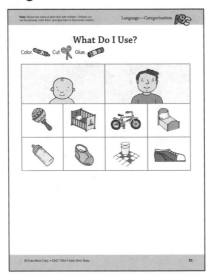

Page 43

Page 44

Page 45

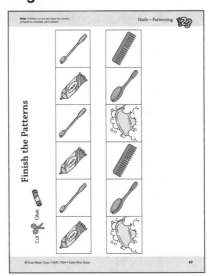

Page 47

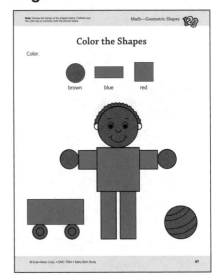